Where Does Your Time Machine Go?

by Ms. Donlin's class
with Tony Stead

capstone

Introduction

Suppose that you could hop in a time machine and instantly travel backward to visit another time and place. Where would you like to go? Perhaps you are an inventor and want to see what life was like during one of the biggest industrial revolutions of our time? Or maybe you'd like to visit a bustling market place to buy goods for your family as you listen to the sounds of pyramid construction in the background. Or maybe you would like to know what it was like to land on the moon! Our class has been studying history, and we thought about what it would be like to actually visit these times long ago and faraway. What would we notice? What would we learn? Follow us on our journey throughout history!

Where Our Time Machines Go

- Ancient Egypt 3100 BC–332 BC
- Colonial America 1492–1775
- Revolutionary War 1775–1783
- Industrial Revolution 1760–1840
- California Gold Rush 1848–1858
- American slavery 1619–1865
- Segregation 1849–1954
- Moon landing July 20, 1969

Ancient Egypt

by Daisy and Noah

I step out of my time machine and see towering pyramids. They're as tall as skyscrapers and a sandy color. I hear a loud "CLANG! CLANG!" I take a look around and see hundreds of people working. They are building huge pyramids. I realized then that I was in ancient Egypt! I may not know the exact year, but I did know that some of these huge pyramids were built more than 5,000 years ago.

The ancient Egyptians built pyramids as tombs for the pharaohs and their queens. The most famous Egyptian pyramids are those found at Giza, outside of Cairo. The pyramids these men were building were COLOSSAL! To make these very large tombs, they used stone from around the area. Some came from far away. The stone was cut into blocks. If the pieces of stone didn't fit, the stones had to be recut.

The workers layered the pyramids by building stairs. Each time they built another level, they had to build more stairs to get there. Wooden sleds made it easier to pull the stones from the ground to the top. I thought it was slaves who built the pyramids. But most people now believe that is a myth. The pyramids were probably made by workers who were paid.

The richest man in ancient Egypt was literally covered in gold from head to foot. This was the pharaoh. Pharaohs were thought of as both man and god. In fact, pharaohs were said to be able to speak to the gods directly. At first, only men could be pharaohs. Hatshepsut was the first woman to be pharaoh. The pharaoh was the most powerful person in ancient Egypt. He or she owned all of the land, made the laws, collected taxes, and protected Egypt against enemies. Many pharaohs went to war when their land was threatened or when they wanted to control foreign lands.

One famous pharaoh was King Tut. He was actually about my age when he became pharaoh, which explains why he was called the "Boy King." His real name was Tutankhamun. I was shocked to learn that he became pharaoh at about 8 years old and that he ruled Egypt for 10 years! Sadly he died at the young age of 19. His body was mummified, which was how ancient Egyptians preserved their royal dead. His golden coffin was buried in a tomb in the Valley of the Kings. In his tomb were lots of jewelry, statues, and weapons. King Tut was one of the most famous kings of ancient Egypt.

It was getting really hot, so I was more than ready to head out of ancient Egypt. It had been an amazing day seeing people and sights up close that I had only read about in history books.

Walking through Colonial Boston in 1773

by Savannah

Where was I now? My time machine had landed in a warm, cozy home. I take a closer look around. The house does not have any electronic lights—just candles and a fire in the brick-covered fireplace. There is a table by the fireplace. I see a newspaper and pick it up. It is titled the *Boston Gazette*. The date is November 1, 1773. I was in Colonial Boston! I quickly realize that this was a crucial time in history with major events taking place!

During this time, King George III was in charge of the colonies. He lived in England, which was across the ocean. American colonists were angry with the king. From their point of view, all he did was tax them for the things they enjoyed, such as tea. The British Parliament taxed the colonists so they could pay back money they owed. The British did not mean to make the colonists angry. However, the colonists were still furious. Men would gather to protest, or demonstrate against, the king's unfair rule.

During Britain's rule, colonists found their own ways to live. Farming and working in a trade were just some of the types of work colonists did to survive. For example, a blacksmith is someone who makes things from iron by hand. A blacksmith could make a horseshoe. Blacksmiths could also make tools such as axe heads, hammers, and plow shares. Paul Revere was a popular blacksmith in Colonial Boston. His shop made spoons, cups, trays, bowls, buttons, and even some coins.

Colonists also started different types of schools. Young boys would attend dame schools. A dame school was an early learning school where children would learn English. This type of school was private and usually taught by women. Dame schools were often in the teacher's home and only boys went to it. Students woke up early, did chores around the house, and went to school. Children were taught the alphabet, Bible verses, and some mathematics. That's a busy day!

During my visit in Colonial Boston, I saw everyone entering and exiting different kinds of shops, and it seemed like they were in a rush to go home. It must be dinnertime because the sun has set. I could smell the food that people were cooking over their fires. It was making me hungry. I headed back to my time machine and was thankful for this experience to walk on the cobblestone streets of Colonial Boston.

Colonial Boston, Massachusetts, was an important center for trade and culture.

The Time of the American Revolution

By Nick

All of a sudden I was back in the 1700s. I noticed right away that life was really different than it is now. I found myself riding on a horse on a bumpy, narrow road. I passed a stagecoach carrying people. The men were wearing tricorn hats, which are hats with three corners that are turned up on three sides. The women had on long dresses with aprons, and the littlest children, both boys and girls, wore a kind of dress called a frock. I was on my way to Boston. I wanted to be part of the action that was happening there and decided to stay for a few years.

In March 1770, Bostonians experienced a terrible tragedy called the Boston Massacre. In this massacre, Crispus Attucks got killed. Here's what happened. Crispus Attucks was a runaway slave from Farmingham, Massachusetts. One night when Crispus got done with his job as a ropemaker, he led a group of sailors to protest against the British soldiers in Boston. The soldiers were in Boston to make sure the colonists followed the king's laws, such as paying his taxes. They started teasing a British guard near the British Customs House. Then some British Redcoats came by and tried to defend their friend. A fight broke out. Some people threw snowballs but others started shooting guns. Crispus Attucks was the first of five men to get killed and is considered the first casualty, or victim, of the American Revolution.

Site of the Boston Massacre

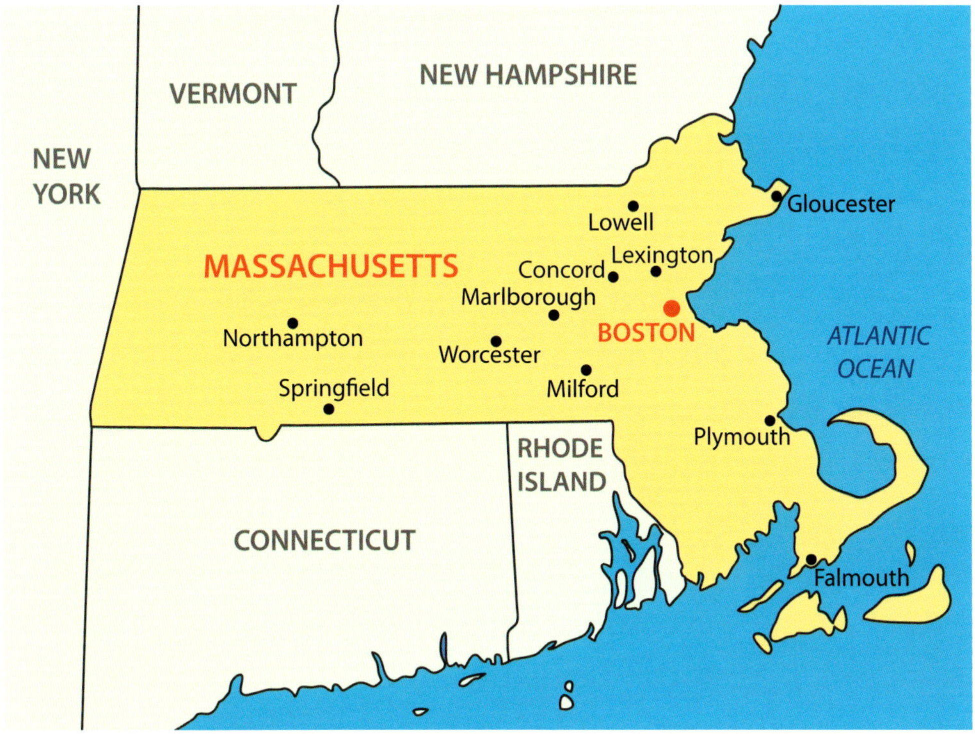

The Boston Massacre took place on the corner of the Devonshire and State streets in downtown Boston.

Later, in December 1773, the American colonists were even angrier with the British. They were not pleased with the way King George III put a tax on practically everything. On a really cold, dark night in Boston, a group of colonists dressed up as Mohawk American Indians. They had gotten onto three British ships anchored there. They threw crates of tea into the water. King George III wanted the colonists to only buy British tea, and it was much too expensive. The colonists were fighting back. Of course, this made the king mad, and he closed the port of Boston until the colonists paid for the tea. All of this trouble led to war.

In April 1775 a spy named Paul Revere became a hero. He was considered a hero because he rode his horse all the way from Boston to Lexington and Concord, telling colonists that the British were coming. In fact, this was when the Battles of Lexington and Concord happened. The colonists, called Patriots, were outnumbered by the British, and the Patriots were not well trained at all. They were mostly farmers. But the British were trained. They even had fancy red uniforms called redcoats. In the first battle, there were many casualties. But then the British went on to Concord and the Patriot soldiers ran into the British on a bridge, which is where the next battle broke out. Believe it or not, the Patriots defeated the British in this battle.

I was worried for America and where it was headed in the 1770s. Many times it seemed like the colonies would lose the war with Britain. But they had declared their independence and eventually became a free nation. How long would their independence last? I think we all can answer that question.

The Industrial Revolution

By Jacob

Booooom! My time machine lands, and I take a look around. A factory's tall chimneys have smoke rising from them. I squint and take a closer look at the sign hanging outside of the building. "James Hargreaves" it says. Thinking back to a textbook I read, I remember that James Hargreaves was famous for inventing the spinning engine in Britain in the 1760s. I make the connection and realize that I am in England in the time period of the Industrial Revolution.

For thousands of years people have had to make things by hand. They also used animals for transportation and to help them with jobs like farming. In the 1700s inventions helped change the world. One example was the steam engine, which uses steam to power machines. Another invention was the flying shuttle. It helped people weave fabric on machines more quickly. With the inventions of the Industrial Revolution, people made fewer things by hand and the machines could finish the work much faster.

Machines were made and used in factories. Children and women were taken away from their own families to work in factories. They had no choice. Some children died because of the deadly conditions of working in the factories. The Watt Steam Engine was an example of this kind of invention. It was made from iron and runs on coal for fuel. This was a great invention for travel, but it could be a deadly weapon. It was very dangerous because the boilers could explode out of nowhere. The water wheel was not so dangerous. This machine was used to power machines.

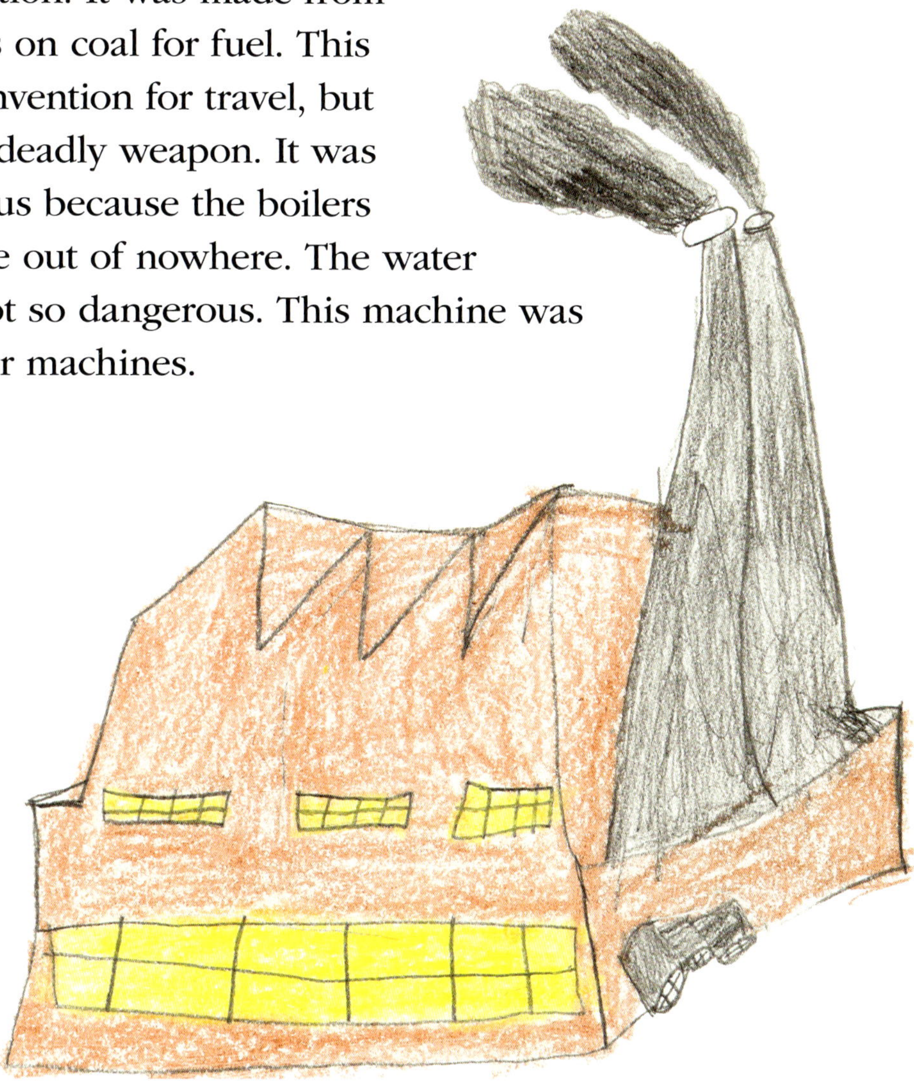

Children started working as young as 6 years old. Can you believe that they worked hard for about 12 to 14 hours or more a day? What's worse is that it was for very little money. Sometimes, if they were lucky, they got one hour for a break. But they usually had to use their break to clean their machines. Not only did the children have working days, but they also had terrible working conditions. Children worked with dangerous equipment, and orphans were treated like slaves. The Factory Act passed in 1833 by Parliament, Britain's lawmaking body, protected kids. Children had to be a certain age to work in factories. Children who were 13 and older could work 12 hours, but children who were younger than 9 did not have to work. This was helpful when it came to a child's health. The United States passed a child labor amendment in 1924.

Regardless of the hardships, this time period had a huge impact on the production and the quality of goods. As I am headed back to the time machine, I stop to wonder who invented this futuristic mode of transportation. What impact would it have had during the Industrial Revolution? Well, now it's back to the time machine to see where I am headed next.

Children worked in the spinning room of the Cornell Mill in Fall River, Massachusetts, in 1912.

The California Gold Rush

By Makhai

My time machine dropped me by the side of a stream. I could hear something that sounded like feet trampling. I turned around and saw thousands of people running toward me shouting, "Gold!" They were carrying pick axes, pans, and shovels. I am in California. It must be about 1849, which was the time of the Gold Rush.

James Wilson Marshall, one of the workers at John Sutter's sawmill, found some shiny flakes of gold in the river near the mill. Sutter and Marshall wanted to keep it a secret, but people found out anyway. Soon prospectors were rushing to California so they could get rich. In fact by 1849 nearly 100,000 people had come to California hoping to find gold. They became known as the 49ers, and they came from all around the world, not just America.

Many of the prospectors did not make a lot of money panning for gold. It was called "panning" for gold because the miners needed a pan. A miner used a shovel to dig down into the river or stream and bring up gravel. The miner put the gravel in the pan and shook it. Because gold is heavy, it eventually sunk to the bottom. Then the miner could take out the gold and set it aside.

The 49ers often lived in boomtowns. These towns grew very quickly when gold was discovered nearby and lots of people moved there all of a sudden. Boomtowns were busy places with lots of stores for people to buy mining supplies. San Francisco was once a boomtown before it became a big city. Some boomtowns died out when the gold ran out and prospectors left. These came to be known as ghost towns because they had abandoned buildings that looked sad and forlorn.

In the end, I'm not sure I wanted to stay in 1849. Life looking for gold was hard and most prospectors never got rich looking for gold that way. I decided to get back to my time machine and leave the Gold Rush.

In the Time of Jackie Robinson

By Jaden

Vroom! I look around and see a bus passing with baseball players. It was the Brooklyn Dodgers. I find a newspaper and look at the date. It is April 11, 1947. On the front page, I read, "Dodgers Purchase Robinson, First Negro in Modern Major League Baseball." This was a big deal.

In this time period, America was a segregated country. That means people were separated because of their skin color. Schools were strictly segregated, which meant that white kids went to one school and black kids went to another one. In some parts of America, especially in the South, restaurants and even drinking fountains were segregated, too. Can you imagine not being able to get a drink of water just because of your skin color? This was a really hard time for African-Americans in this country. Even if you were a great baseball player, you could not play on a major sports team. The Dodgers manager Branch Rickey began to change all this when he asked Jackie Robinson to play baseball for the Brooklyn Dodgers.

Stop
The New York Times
April 11, 1947
Dodgers Purchase
Robinson

In the Dodger Stadium most of the crowd booed Jackie and threw stuff at him like cans and trash. In one game, Jackie Robinson was finally up at bat. It was the eighth inning. People screamed mean insults. Branch Rickey was afraid that Jackie Robinson would fight back. Jackie swung at the ball and hit it to center field. He stole second. The pitcher threw wide, and Jackie made it home! The crowd cheered. Jackie helped to save the day for his team.

I think to myself, "Wow! Jackie Robinson had a huge impact on sports. He always stood up for what was right." I wonder how much strength it took for him to ignore the yells and threats. Due to Jackie Robinson's bravery and talent, baseball was an integrated sport after Jackie paved the way.

Jackie Robinson was up to bat during a game in 1948.

A Time for Change

by Daisy

Bump! All of a sudden, I was on a moving bus. I looked out the window and saw trees and houses. I also saw a sign with "Montgomery" on it. I looked around the bus. Ahead of me were only white people. I turned around and saw only African-Americans. I was stunned to realize I was in the time period of segregation.

During the 1950s most of America was segregated. This meant that people went to different schools and public places because of their different races. Many people tried to end segregation. The African-Americans wanted equal rights. More and more people began speaking up for themselves. But there were laws in place that only helped segregation.

The Jim Crow laws took place in Southern states. The Jim Crow laws were bad for African-Americans. These were laws that separated black people from white people. These laws led to mobs and sometimes led to African-Americans being killed. People were killed even if they were innocent. These laws angered many people.

Due to the segregation in the 1950s, more people started to stand up for their rights. Rosa Parks was one example. She was supposed to give up her seat on a bus to a white man, but she wouldn't do it. Her actions helped motivate people to stand up for themselves. After that event, 40,000 African-Americans walked for 381 days. They didn't ride the buses. Finally, the Supreme Court ended bus segregation. Rosa Parks was a symbol of equality. Her goal was to have freedom for all people.

I didn't see Rosa Parks when I traveled back to that time period, but I was glad to know a little more about her. She and other people, such as Dr. Martin Luther King Jr., helped fight for equal rights. Life would be different now if it weren't for Rosa Parks and Dr. Martin Luther King Jr.

Space Travel's Big Impact

by Emma

Zap! Suddenly it was 1969. I land on a strange place. It is a gray color, and it is surrounded by a pitch black sky with gleaming stars. I come to the conclusion that I'm on the moon! I look down, and I have a space suit on. I also have a helmet on my head and a tank on my back. The tank is for oxygen so I can breathe because there is no oxygen on the moon. I look over and see men near the American flag. I noticed the men were Neil Armstrong and Edwin Aldrin!

It was July 20, 1969, when Neil Armstrong and two other astronauts flew to the moon in the spaceship *Apollo 11.* Armstrong opened the doors for humans exploring space. First came Sputnik, a satellite launched by Russia on October 4, 1957. It was about the size of a beach ball and took about 98 minutes to orbit Earth. Sputnik had caught America off guard in the competition to space that America and Russia were having. Luckily for America, on January 31, 1958, things turned around. America launched the satellite *Explorer 1* into space.

1969

The astronauts communicated with NASA by radio signal. NASA helped them to get to the moon and land safely. They also helped them with any problems with the ship, such as a computer problem that happened just before the spaceship touched down on the moon. Neil Armstrong's famous words when he walked onto the moon were, "That's one small step for man; One giant leap for mankind."

America was the first country to send men to the moon. Everything was going well until January 1986. There was going to be another space flight and everyone was excited because a teacher was going to go on this mission. The spaceship was the *Challenger*. The teacher's name was Christa McAuliffe. She was going to teach kids while flying around space. But there was a huge crisis. The O-rings failed, which means the rocket booster didn't separate. The *Challenger* exploded on takeoff, and all seven astronauts were killed immediately. Due to this problem, all space shuttle missions stopped for a while.

Before I start to walk back to the time machine, I take one last look around. I look at the silvery stars and the dusty ground. It was fun going to the moon. I wish I knew more about it. I hop in the time machine and *Zap!* I'm home again. I'm so tired my eyes close, and I'm instantly asleep.

Buzz Aldrin stands next to the U.S. flag during the first moon landing.

Conclusion

What can we learn from traveling through history? We found out about ancient Egypt, Colonial Boston, the Industrial Revolution, segregation in America, and the time of the moon landing. We learned a lot of lessons from looking at what happened in the past, both good and bad. While these historical times are all different, one thing about them is the same—they are all interesting to study! Where would you go in YOUR time machine?

illustrated by Emma